W9-BTA-498

Jim Arnosky

Shimmer & Splash

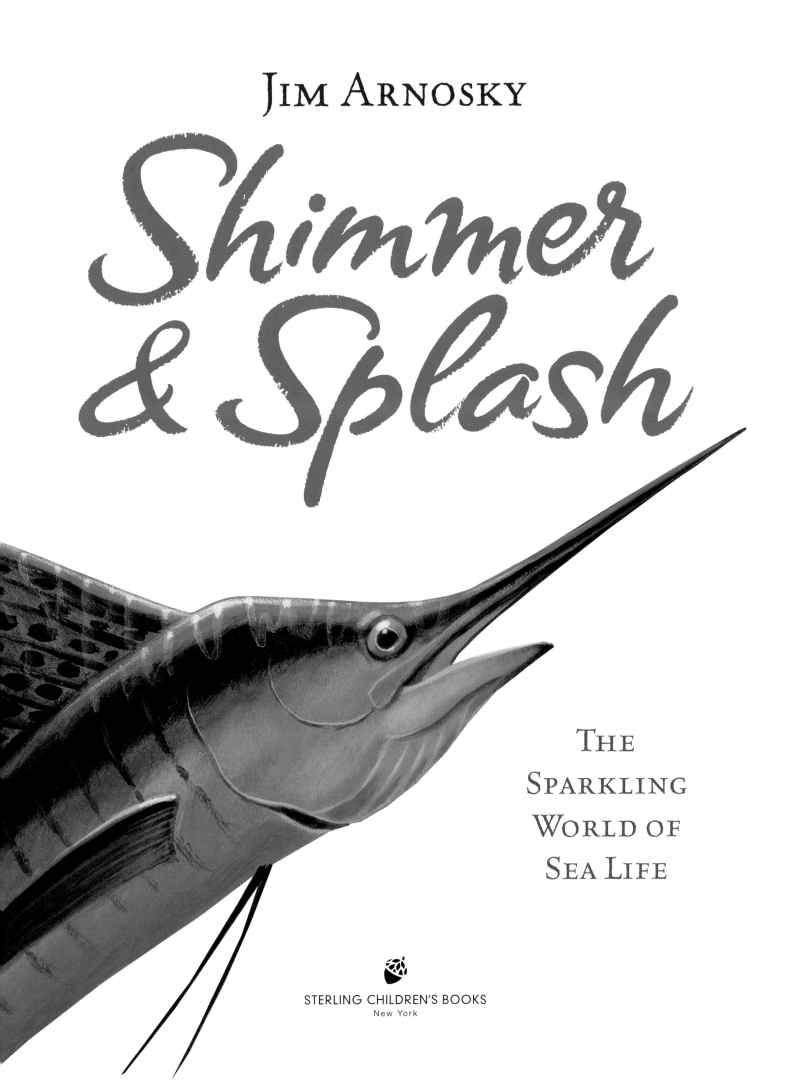

The Sparkling World of Sea Life

STERLING CHILDREN'S BOOKS
New York

FOR RICK AND NANCY

STERLING CHILDREN'S BOOKS
New York

An Imprint of Sterling Publishing
387 Park Avenue South
New York, NY 10016

STERLING CHILDREN'S BOOKS and the distinctive
Sterling Children's Books logo are trademarks of Sterling Publishing Co., Inc.

© 2013 by Jim Arnosky

Display lettering created by Georgia Deaver
Design by Elizabeth Phillips
The artwork for this book was prepared using pencil and acrylic paints.

All rights reserved. No part of this publication may be reproduced, stored in
a retrieval system, or transmitted, in any form or by any means, electronic,
mechanical, photocopying, recording, or otherwise, without prior written
permission from the publisher.

ISBN 978-1-4027-8623-5

Library of Congress Cataloging-in-Publication Data

Arnosky, Jim
  Shimmer and splash : the sparkling world of sea life / Jim Arnosky.
    p. cm.
  ISBN 978-1-4027-8623-5 (hardcover)
  1. Marine animals--Juvenile literature. I. Title.
  QL122.2.A76 2013
  591.77--dc23
                    2012012863

Distributed in Canada by Sterling Publishing
c/o Canadian Manda Group, 165 Dufferin Street
Toronto, Ontario, Canada M6K 3H6
Distributed in the United Kingdom by GMC Distribution Services
Castle Place, 166 High Street, Lewes, East Sussex, England BN7 1XU
Distributed in Australia by Capricorn Link (Australia) Pty. Ltd.
P.O. Box 704, Windsor, NSW 2756, Australia

For information about custom editions, special sales, and premium and
corporate purchases, please contact Sterling Special Sales at 800-805-5489
or specialsales@sterlingpublishing.com.

Manufactured in China
Lot #:
2 4 6 8 10 9 7 5 3 1
11/12

www.sterlingpublishing.com/kids

CONTENTS

BLUE MARLIN

Introduction

The ocean is a wilderness that remains mostly unexplored.
Step in the surf and you are entering a waterworld where
you can spend a lifetime trying to learn the names of all the
inhabitants. I came to the sea to find the fish; to cast my line into
the blue, hoping to reel in another story to tell, along with a fish.
In the process, I became hooked on the beauty of the water, the
rhythm of the tides, and the seemingly endless variety of sea life.

I wondered what it would be like to live in the sea, and I
learned as much as I could about every creature I encountered.
My wildlife journals quickly filled with sketches and notes of
animals entirely new to me. I had found a naturalist's paradise.

This book focuses on sea life that can easily be seen in the
shallow water near the beaches or just offshore where, from the
deck of a boat, some spectacular marine species patrol the deeper
water. From jetties and shores and fishing boats, my wife, Deanna,
and I searched for marine life and every day some new fish or other
creature found its way into my book.

Here are my sea stories and paintings of the ocean dwellers that
inspired them. Each section begins with a particular sea creature
that serves as a start to look at more of its kind or other marine
animals that share the same habitat. Wherever I could, I painted
the actual sizes of the species or I've noted maximum lengths and
weights. But even the largest of them is just one small speck of life
in the vastness of the sea.

Jim Arnosky

BONNETHEAD
SHARK

SHARPNOSE
PUFFER

To avoid being swallowed by
larger fish, a puffer will inflate
itself with water or air and swell
up like a balloon.

BARRACUDA

INSHORE HUNTERS

In the ocean, the water doesn't have to be deep for a watchful wader to see a variety of fish, including some large and spectacular ones. Shallow sunlit water is a hunting ground for big fish that feed on crabs and small fish. Here are some of the inshore hunters I have encountered while wading knee-deep in clear water.

ATLANTIC
NEEDLEFISH

All of the fish are
shown average size.
They can grow to
be two to three
times larger.

SPOTTED EAGLE RAY

BOTTLENOSE DOLPHIN

BONEFISH

TARPON

PERMIT

Stingrays

I was wading near the shoreline when I spotted a dark spot on the otherwise bright sandy bottom. I took another few steps, shuffling my feet to warn of my approach just in case it was a stingray hiding. Stingrays ambush small fish by burying themselves in the sand. I took another cautious step and suddenly the dark spot materialized into a large southern stingray that raced away, leaving a blur of sand in its wake.

Anyone looking for sea life in the shallows also needs to know what to look out for. By looking out for stingrays, I also become aware of everything else in the shallow water.

A stingray is a flat-bodied, cartilaginous fish, which means its skeleton is made of highly flexible cartilage rather than bone. Rays have huge pectoral (side) fins resembling wings that they flap to fly slowly through the water or power themselves away from danger. Danger to a stingray is a shark that may want to eat it or a human who might accidently step on it. Stingrays can defend themselves by means of a sharp poisonous spine located at the base of the ray's long whip-like tail. The sting of a stingray is very painful.

Stingrays come in a variety of shapes and sizes, depending on the species. The round stingray has a "wingspan" of two feet. The triangular-shaped southern stingray and cownose ray each have wingspans of three feet. The most beautiful stingray Deanna and I have ever seen is the spotted eagle ray, which has a wingspan of up to ten feet. These large rays glide over rocky and sandy bottoms in search of shrimp and shellfish to suck up and crush in their strong-jawed mouths. I have seen round, southern, cownose, and eagle rays all in less than three feet of water.

When buried under sand, a stingray breathes through the blowholes located behind its eyes.

Dolphins

We were heading back to land after a sunny afternoon out on the water. I pushed the boat's throttle to make us go faster and suddenly Deanna shouted, "We have company!" A pod of bottlenose dolphins was swimming behind the boat, leaping and splashing in our wake. I changed directions to get out of their way, but the dolphins stayed with us, speeding along, weaving back and forth in our water trail. I turned again. They followed, and kept following until I slowed to a crawl upon approaching the shore. Only then did the dolphins finally swim away.

Dolphins love to leap and play in the water. Their obvious intelligence makes me wonder how they think, and what they know. Like us, dolphins are mammals. They breathe through a blowhole on top of their heads. Many people see them as kindred spirits—friendly, peaceful, and non-aggressive. But to the fish of the sea, dolphins are dangerous ocean predators.

I once watched a pair of dolphins feeding on a school of small fish close to shore. Whole showers of fleeing fish leaped out of the water, frantic to escape. The dolphins sped back and forth, turning every which way to corral and snap up their terrified prey. When some of the fish leaped right out of the surf and landed flopping on the beach, the dolphins skidded out onto the wet sand to gobble them up. Then they wriggled back into the surf to chase some more.

Dolphins and whales have horizontal tails.

Fish tails are vertical.

Actual Size

A dolphin's peg-like teeth are for puncturing tough fish scales.

Dolphins are sometimes mistaken for sharks. I always look for the rounded tip of a dolphin's dorsal fin and the dolphin's undulating motion.

DOLPHIN

SHARK

13

The dolphins we see near shore are usually bottlenose dolphins. They are shallow water dwellers, and can be found in the Atlantic and Pacific Oceans. Depending on the light, they look gray, brown, or black in color. They grow to be twelve feet long and have no distinctive markings. The most colorful and strikingly marked dolphins are found offshore. Deepwater dolphins spend their lives far from land. I thought you might like to see what some of them look like.

COMMON DOLPHIN
Length: 9 feet
Atlantic and Pacific Oceans

KILLER WHALE
Length: 31 feet
Atlantic and Pacific Oceans
as far south as the Equator

Killer whale is a name derived from "whale killer," a nickname given by early sailors who sometimes saw them attacking and killing whales. The killer whale is actually the largest member of the dolphin family, and is also known by the name orca. All dolphins eat fish. Killer whales also eat seals, sea birds, and sea turtles.

Rough-Toothed Dolphin

Length: 9 feet
Atlantic and Pacific Oceans

Striped Dolphin

Length: 8 feet
Tropical Atlantic and Pacific Oceans

Pacific White-Sided Dolphin

Length: 9 feet
Pacific Ocean

Like fish, dolphins and whales have dorsal fins.
But where fish have pectoral (side) fins, dolphins
and whales have flat paddle-like limbs called flippers.

MAN-O-WAR AND MOON JELLYFISH

Jellyfish

During high tide, jellyfish and other drifting sea creatures sometimes wash ashore. If you see globs of clear jelly lying on the beach, these are jellyfish stranded by the receding tide. If you see what look like small inflated blue balloons lying on the sand or floating in the surf, those are man-o-war—animals very similar to jellyfish. Be careful not to touch them or step on them!

Jellyfish and man-o-war have tentacles that snag, sting, and paralyze small sea animals. To humans, the stings of most jellyfish are mild and can be treated with a wipe of alcohol, which dissolves the tiny poisonous barbs left by the creatures' tentacles. However, the stings of some jellyfish, such as the lion's mane jellyfish found in the Atlantic Ocean and the box jellyfish found in the Indian Ocean, are so toxic they can kill a person. The sting of a man-o-war is not lethal but the pain is long-lasting and can only be relieved very slowly by repeated gentle washings with warm water.

When I'm wading in the ocean and see a jellyfish or man-o-war drifting toward me, I step away and watch as it goes by. These animals are as beautiful as they are dangerous.

Some jellyfish such as the moon jellyfish and upside-down jellyfish can swim from place to place by undulating their bodies. They feed by constantly filtering sea water to trap tiny particles of food. Lion's mane jellyfish and man-o-war depend on the ocean's current to move them from place to place.

Lion's Mane Jellyfish

Upside-down Jellyfish

Box Jellyfish

A ten-inch man-o-war can be dragging five feet of tentacles. The lion's mane jellyfish has six feet of tentacles. Box jellyfish have tentacles that can reach ten feet. These free-floating predators have downward facing mouths into which they pull paralyzed prey.

17

ALBACORE
(a small species of tuna)

Billfish attack schools of smaller fish by circling them and then lunging into the school, using their long bills to slash and stun the fish before gobbling them up.

Sailfish have the added advantage of using their large "sails" (dorsal fins) to corral and contain a school of fish before slashing through it.

BLUE MARLIN
Length: 15 feet
Weight: 1,200 pounds
Various subspecies of marlin can be found in the Atlantic and Pacific Oceans

SAILFISH

Sailfish

Sailfish are not the kind of fish you see in aquariums. Their long sword-like bills make them too dangerous to keep in captivity. The only way to see one of these magnificent creatures is by going out on the ocean and actually reeling one in, or catching a glimpse of one swimming near the surface. Either way requires a big boat and a considerable amount of luck. The only sailfish I have ever seen in the wild were leaping high out of the waves after flying fish (fish whose long pectoral fins enable them to glide on air), or swimming near our boat, flashing their long silver sides just under the waves.

Sailfish are named after their large dorsal fin which, when raised, resembles a ship's sail. These fish can grow to be ten feet long and weigh over two hundred pounds. They are the smallest members of the awesome billfish family, which also includes marlin and swordfish.

Sailfish and Flying fish

Sailfish, marlin, and swordfish are large, streamlined fish with long, pointed bills. All three can be recognized at a glance by the shape of their dorsal fins.

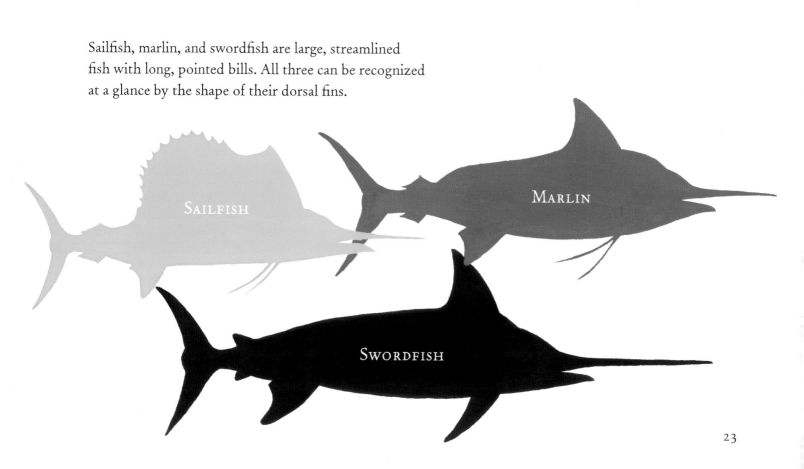

SAILFISH

MARLIN

SWORDFISH

23

WAHOO

At seven feet in length and almost two hundred pounds, wahoos are among the largest members in the mackerel family, surpassed only by the big tuna.

DEEP-SEA HUNTERS

Fish such as marlin that live in the open ocean, far from land, are called pelagic fish. Pelagic means "the sea." Since people rarely see them, their lives are mostly mysterious. Here are five pelagic fish and some things that we know about them.

DOLPHIN FISH (MAHI)

Dolphins, such as the bottlenose dolphin, are mammals. But there are also fish called dolphins. Dolphin fish are also known as dorado or mahi, and these fish grow very quickly from tiny fry to as large as six feet in length. They can weigh over eighty pounds.

SWORDFISH

Swordfish swim in schools at depths of more than two thousand feet. Swordfish can grow to be fourteen feet long (including the bill) and weigh over a thousand pounds.

BIG-EYE THRESHER SHARK

All thresher sharks have super-long tails that they use to clobber schools of small fish before eating them. This fantastic species can grow to be twenty-five feet long and weigh eight hundred pounds.

YELLOWFIN TUNA

At seven feet in length and four hundred pounds, the yellowfin tuna is one of the largest, heaviest, and most powerful of all the members of the mackerel family. Like all tuna, yellowfins travel in large schools and are highly sought after for food. Most of the tuna we eat are yellowfin tuna.

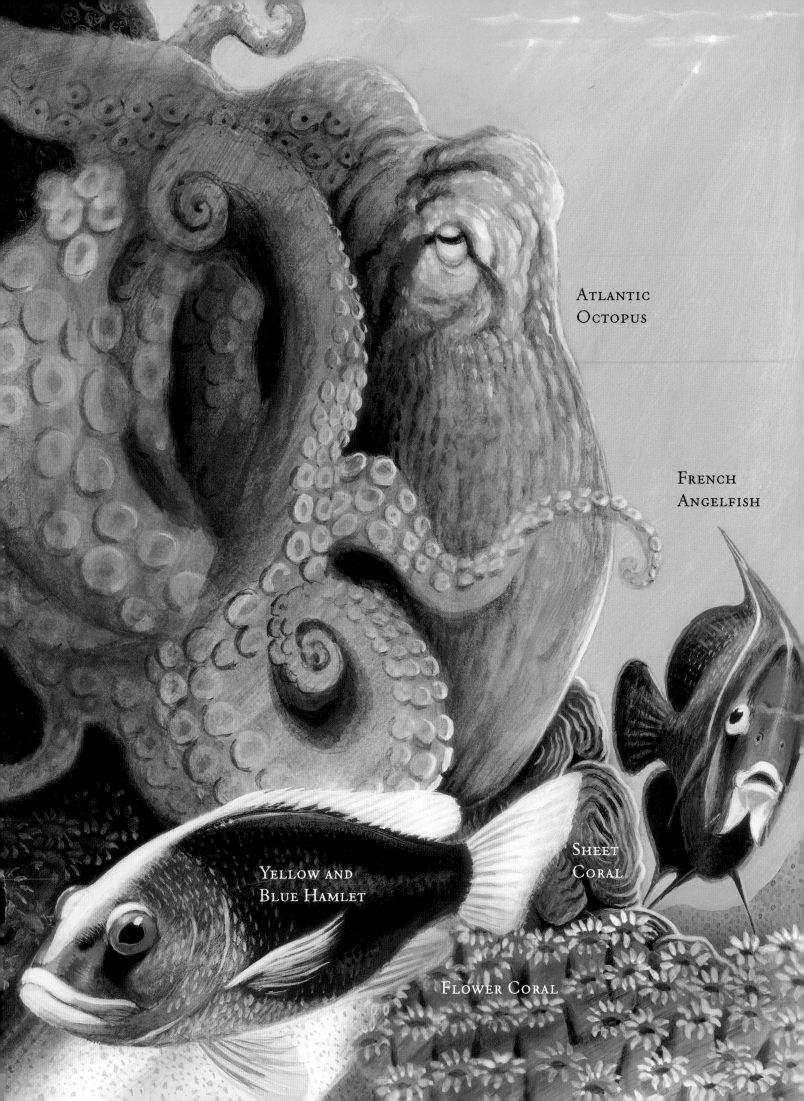

ATLANTIC
OCTOPUS

FRENCH
ANGELFISH

SHEET
CORAL

YELLOW AND
BLUE HAMLET

FLOWER CORAL

Coral Reef

In the ocean, between shallow inshore water and the open sea, parts of the bottom stand higher than the rest of the sea floor, forming lumps, bumps, or jagged ridges. These high places are called reefs. They can be made of rock or coral or both.

A coral reef is a living thing made up of tiny coral animals called polyps that, joined together, resemble either rocks or plants. Float slowly over a coral reef and you see coral fans waving gently in the current like large leaves blowing in the wind. Coral branches reach upward in the water like the branches of trees. And mounds of hard coral sit like rocks on the sandy sea floor.

Corals live and die, and as new generations of corals grow on the calcified (hard) skeletons of the old, the reef increases in height until its top ridge is just beneath the surface of the waves. Before offshore lighthouses were built to warn mariners of this hidden danger, many ships were lost as they crashed against the jagged reefs.

A coral reef can be one long mass that stretches hundreds of miles, or it can be made up of many small separate "patch reefs." There are cold-water reefs that form on the ocean floor miles beneath the waves, and stand as tall as the buildings in a large city.

Most coral reefs, however, are found in shallow tropical waters, awash with sunlight and inhabited by brightly colored fish. The variety and diversity of marine animals that live in tropical coral reefs is greater than anywhere else in the ocean.

Three Soft Corals

Corky sea fingers

Sea fan

Sea rod

Three Hard Corals

Rose coral

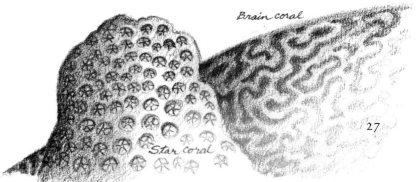

Brain coral

Star coral

27

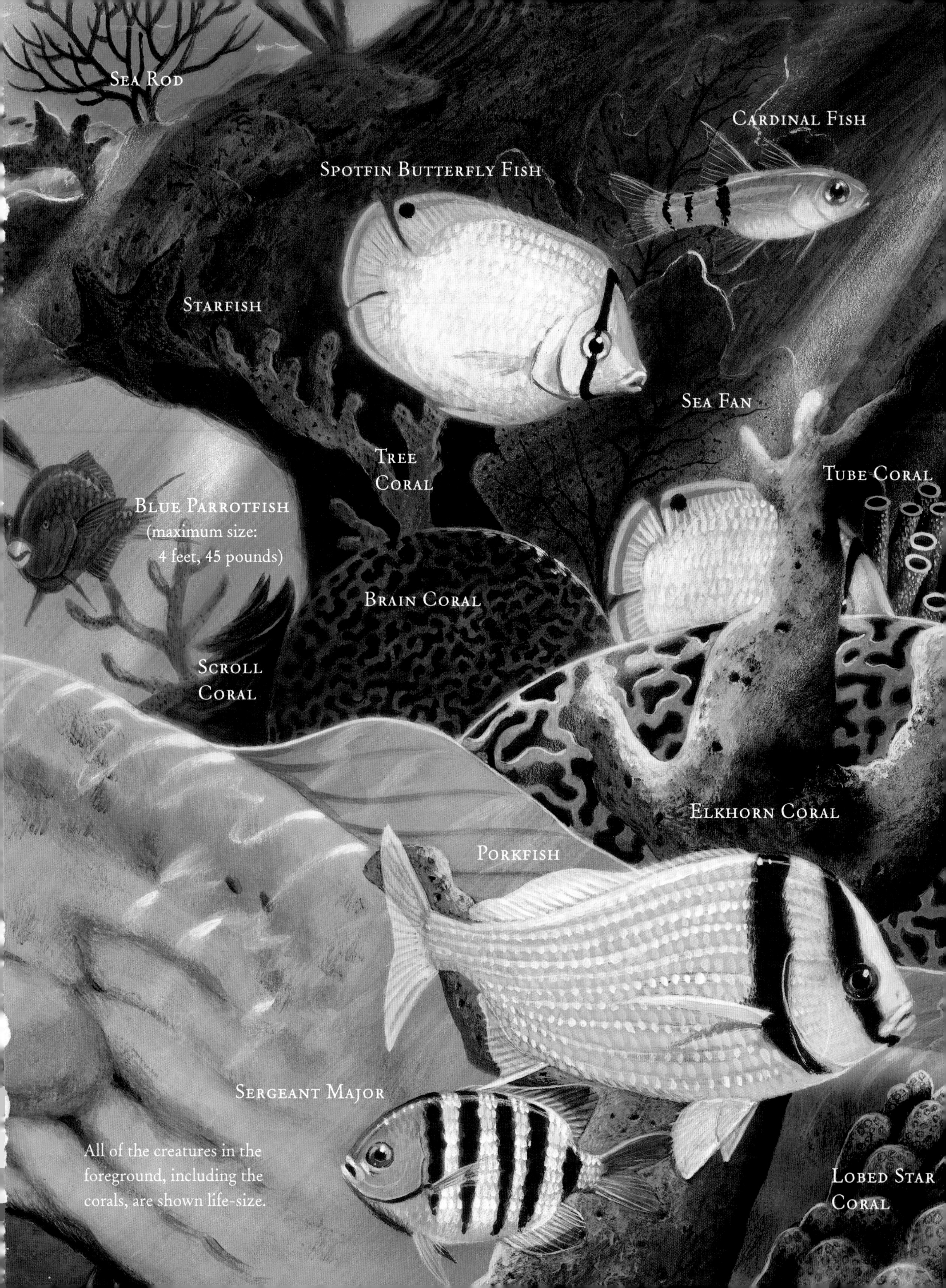

SEA ROD

CARDINAL FISH

SPOTFIN BUTTERFLY FISH

STARFISH

SEA FAN

TUBE CORAL

TREE
CORAL

BLUE PARROTFISH
(maximum size:
4 feet, 45 pounds)

BRAIN CORAL

SCROLL
CORAL

ELKHORN CORAL

PORKFISH

SERGEANT MAJOR

All of the creatures in the
foreground, including the
corals, are shown life-size.

LOBED STAR
CORAL

A coral reef is a veritable underwater city where everything, even the reef itself, is alive. Fish, turtles, and other marine animals that range broadly over the ocean come to the reef to feed on the smaller sea creatures that live and hide in the crevices and holes between the different species of corals or swim in the grooves and gullies in the coral-covered sea floor.

GOLIATH GROUPER
(maximum size: 11 feet, 700 pounds)

GREEN TURTLE
(maximum size: 3 feet, 100 pounds)

GREEN MORAY EEL
(maximum size: 8 feet, 65 pounds)

DAMSELFISH

CORAL CRAB

KNOBBY
BRAIN
CORAL

LEAF
CORAL

BLUEHEAD

CACTUS CORAL

MANATEE, SHEEPSHEAD FISH,
AND MANGROVE SNAPPERS

A Good Place to Be

The ocean is vast and deep. Even the largest of fish and the greatest of whales are small in comparison. Except for color change—green near shore, cobalt offshore, and blue-black in the depths, there is a sameness to the water, mile after mile after mile. Fish are attracted to any difference in temperature and water clarity. Reefs and ledges draw them. Even the slightest feature on the sea floor—a rock, sponge, or hump of sand, can become a fish hangout.

In the open ocean, fish congregate under seaweeds, discarded wooden boards, and sheets of old plywood floating on the surface. A single lost buoy becomes an attraction for small sea creatures and a favorite hunting place for larger ones.

Great big slow-moving animals such as whale sharks and manta rays often have a population of small fish swimming in the shade their huge bodies cast in the water. On Florida's southern coast, where mangrove trees stand on their sturdy roots in salty water, Deanna and I watched a manatee swimming with a crowd of mangrove snappers and striped sheepshead schooling beneath it. They were staying cool in the manatee's shadow and feeding on the minnows attracted to the algae and other organisms growing on the manatee's skin. The fish were also keeping safe by swimming together close to their enormous host. For a small fish in a sea full of large predators, it was a good place to be.

Life under a lost buoy.

The tiny holes on a shark's snout are called ampullae and are sensory pores that detect electrical impulses emitted by other fish. This helps sharks locate prey even in darkness.

GREAT WHITE SHARK
Length: 23 feet
Weight: 2,700 pounds
Surface waters near shore in Atlantic and Pacific Oceans

SHARKS

Like rays, sharks are cartilaginous. A skeleton of flexible cartilage combined with a large, powerful tail and streamlined shape makes a shark an extremely agile predator. Sharks are able to swim fast, turn sharply, and attack rapidly. A shark bite can happen so quickly that there is often little or no time to escape the fearsome teeth and vice-like jaws.

Shark teeth vary in shape and design from species to species. The teeth of the great white and tiger shark are made for chopping, cutting, and even sawing through the bones of large prey. Others, like the dagger shaped teeth of sand and mako sharks, are perfect for snagging and holding onto swift fleeing fish. Hammerhead shark teeth combine the dagger point with flat, razor-sharp, serrated edges for cutting, and biting off big chunks of flesh.

TOOTH OF AN 18-FOOT GREAT WHITE SHARK
shown actual size

JAWS AND TEETH OF A 10-FOOT TIGER SHARK
shown actual size

MAKO SHARK
Length: 13 feet
Weight: 1,000 pounds
Offshore waters, Atlantic and Pacific Oceans
The tooth shown at left once belonged to a 9-foot
mako shark, and is shown actual size.

BLACKTIP SHARK

Sharks

Of all the creatures in the sea, only the shark can send swimmers scrambling for shore or make seasoned fishermen worry about the size of their boats. I like to fish for sharks for the adventure of it, and to photograph them before carefully returning them—unharmed—to the water.

The biggest shark I've ever photographed this way was reeled in by a friend of mine one spooky, moonlit evening. When the shark first took the bait, we didn't know what it was. It stayed deep, tugging hard and towing our small boat across the dark water. When we finally had the shark beside the boat, we could see that it was a nurse shark, at least eight feet in length, and well over a hundred pounds.

I leaned over the side to get as close as possible and snapped a few pictures. Then the big shark was released and it sank, swimming slowly downward into the blackness.

Nurse sharks could very well be named for the fact that they live their whole lives in the vicinity of the shallow nursery waters where they were born. The actual origin of the name is unknown. Nurse sharks can be identified by their large, rudder-shaped tails. In fact, all of the six major families of sharks can be distinguished by tail shape.

We saw other sharks that night in the moonlight: one lemon shark and the blacktip shark shown on the opposite page. Lemons and blacktips can grow to be eight feet long and weigh about 200 pounds. They belong to the largest family of sharks known as requiem sharks, found in both the Atlantic and Pacific Oceans.

Mackerel Sharks

[Includes Great White and Mako Sharks.]

Sand Tiger Sharks

Requiem Sharks

[Includes Whitetip, Blacktip, Lemon, Tiger, and Bull Sharks.]

Hammerhead Sharks

Thresher Sharks

35

Nurse sharks don't chase prey. They simply suck it up with their wide mouths. Nurse shark teeth are small but strong and are used for crushing and crunching crab and lobster shells.

Nurse Shark
Length: 14 feet
Weight: 500 pounds
Shallow bays and near shore in Atlantic and Pacific Oceans

A nurse shark tooth shown greatly enlarged.

I see nurse sharks while I'm wading. Often one will swim by me quite closely. Snorkelers frequently encounter these non-aggressive sharks and, as long as the snorkeler doesn't reach out and grab them, the sharks remain harmless.

A hammerhead's widespread eyes can see all around and also increase the shark's depth perception for zeroing in on prey.

Tooth of a 10-foot Hammerhead Shark
shown actual size

Sharks have back rows of spare teeth ready to move forward and replace any lost front-row teeth.

TIGER SHARK
Length: 21 feet
Weight: 1,800 pounds
Surface waters near shore in
Atlantic and Pacific Oceans

HAMMERHEAD SHARK
Length: 13 feet
Weight: 1,500 pounds
Surface waters near shore in
Atlantic and Pacific Oceans

FIDDLER CRABS

Male fiddler with large pincher at rest.

Fighting Fiddlers

One day, Deanna and I arrived at the beach at low tide just in time to see two fiddler crabs fighting atop a mound of mud. The fighters, both males distinguished by their one large right pincher, were reaching and snapping their huge claws to grab hold of their opponent. They pushed with their legs, trying to knock one another down. It was a ritual battle to insure that only the strongest of the species would reproduce.

Fiddler crabs are named for the one oversized pincher found only on the males. At rest, the large claw is held against the crab's body the way a violin is held under a player's chin. The big pincher claws look heavy and unwieldy, but I have seen them used delicately to pick up tiny bits and pieces of organic material called detritus, which crabs and lobsters feed on.

Crabs and lobsters are ten-legged animals (decopods) with jointed limbs, segmented bodies, outer skeletons, and powerful abdomens and tails, which can propel the animals quickly through the water.

As a crab or lobster grows, it sheds its outer shell, exposing a new shell beneath. The new shell is soft but hardens rather quickly. The hermit crab is a species with a permanently soft shell. To protect it, the crab climbs inside the empty shell of a snail, whelk, or conch, and carries the impenetrable fortress around. As a hermit crab grows in size, the outgrown borrowed shell is exchanged for a larger one.

Pincher
Parts of a crab
Eye
Carapace
Jointed legs
Abdomen (usually tucked under shell)

Feeler
Carapace
Abdomen
Tail
Lobster

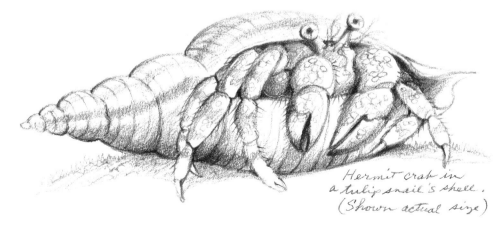
Hermit crab in a tulip snail's shell. (Shown actual size)

PORCUPINE FISH

Waters of Wonder

Most of the life in the sea is concentrated near shore in water less than 100 feet deep. But even the deepest places in the ocean harbor sea creatures swimming in the endless night or burrowing in the dark sand. Some, like the five-inch long chiasmodon and the twelve-inch long viperfish, live exclusively in the abyss, locating one another by means of small spots of glowing light caused by a chemical action in their bodies known as bio-luminescence.

Other deep-sea creatures are not permanent residents. Squid migrate vertically, swimming from the surface to the depths, following the population of plankton—microscopic animals and plants that form the basis of the food chain for sea life of all sizes, including sixty-five-foot-long baleen whales.

Sperm whales dive miles deep to hunt their favorite food, the giant squid. Imagine the battle that goes on in the lightless depths between a seventy-foot sperm whale and a fifty-foot giant squid! Giant squids are denizens of the deep that have only recently been discovered by science. What other giants swim unknown at the bottom of the sea?

The sea expands the limits of our imagination. But whatever we can imagine, the actual life in the sea is bound to be more fantastic! I am always amazed but never surprised when I learn of a newly discovered saltwater animal.

At the end of each day we spend in coastal areas, Deanna and I walk along our favorite beaches and watch the sun go down. We ease into the steady rhythm of the waves, while our thoughts float peacefully away, sailing the distant waters of wonder. The sea cradles many wonders.

Plankton
(Greatly enlarged)

Viperfish

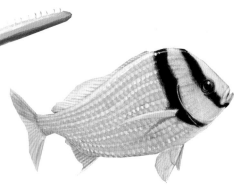

Author's Note

As in all my books, the text and chosen wildlife subjects are guided from real experiences Deanna and I have had in wild places. Much of the narrative comes directly from my journals and notes written fresh from the field.

To research my paintings, we photograph and videotape animals in the wild. We also visit zoos, private preserves, and aquariums to see animals up close. While working on this book I carried a pocket-sized sketch pad and Deanna brought a small digital camera everywhere we went. I sketched some excellent taxidermy mounts of actual fish and beautiful life-sized fiberglass molds of fish hanging on walls. On the beach, whenever we found a fish or octopus swimming in the surf, I took out my pad and sketched for as long as the animal stayed near.

We spent whole days on our little boat, *Crayfish*. I fished, and the fish I caught, Deanna photographed up close before I released them. I fished alone, wading the shallows, and on bigger boats with guides who could take me out to the deep sea to find the species of fish I wanted to see.

Deanna and I paddled in a kayak and floated on our little inflatable dinghy, looking down into the water, wondering about what we saw. All of this research was fun, and helped make *Shimmer and Splash* one of our favorite books. We hope it also becomes a favorite of yours.

More About Sea Life

Arnosky, Jim. *All About Manatees*. New York: Scholastic, 2008.

Arnosky, Jim. *Dolphins on the Sand*. New York: Putnam Juvenile, 2008.

Arnosky, Jim. *Hook, Line, & Seeker: A Beginner's Guide to Fishing, Boating, and Watching Water Wildlife*. New York: Scholastic, 2005.

Chin, Jason. *Coral Reefs*. New York: Flash Point/Roaring Brook Press, 2011.

Cramer, Deborah. *Smithsonian Ocean: Our Water, Our World*. Washington, D.C.: Smithsonian, 2008.

Doubilet, David and Hayes, Jennifer. *Face to Face With Sharks*. Washington, D.C.: National Geographic Children's Books, 2009.

Hynes, Margaret. *Oceans and Seas*. New York: Kingfisher/Macmillan, 2010.

Knowlton, Nancy. *Citizens of the Sea: Wondrous Creatures from the Census of Marine Life*. Washington, D.C.: National Geographic, 2010.

Lourie, Peter. *The Manatee Scientists: Saving Vulnerable Species*. Boston, MA: Houghton Mifflin Books for Children, 2011.

MacQuitty, Miranda. *Eyewitness Expert: Shark*. New York: DK Publishing, 2008.

Mojetta, Angelo. *The Coral Reef*. New York: White Star Publishers/Sterling, 2011.

Parker, Steve. *DK Eyewitness Books: Fish*. New York: DK Publishing, 2005.

Rizzo, Johnna. *Oceans: Dolphins, Sharks, Penguins, and More!* Washington, D.C.: National Geographic Children's Books, 2010.

Siebert, Charles. *The Secret World of Whales*. San Francisco, CA: Chronicle Books, 2011.